SQUEAL AND SQUAWK

BARNYARD TALK

BY **SUSAN PEARSON**

ILLUSTRATED BY
DAVID SLONIM

Marshall Cavendish
New York • London • Singapore

For Ted and Betsy Lewin,
with special thanks to Margery Cuyler
—S. P.

For Jonathan, Daniel, Michael and Mary
—D. S.

Text copyright © 2004 by Susan Pearson
Illustrations copyright © 2004 by David Slonim
All rights reserved

Marshall Cavendish Children's Books
Marshall Cavendish, 99 White Plains Road, Tarrytown, NY 10591
www.marshallcavendish.com

Library of Congress Cataloging-in-Publication Data

Pearson, Susan.
Squeal and squawk : barnyard talk / by Susan Pearson ; illustrated by
David Slonim.-- 1st ed.
p. cm.
Summary: Original poems about barnyard animals.
ISBN 0-7614-5160-9
1. Domestic animals--Juvenile poetry. 2. Children's poetry,
American. I. Slonim, David, ill. II. Title.
PZ7.P323316Sq 2004
811'.54--dc21
2003009111

The text of this book is set in Bernhard Modern.
The illustrations are rendered in reed pen and ink and acrylics.
Book design by Daniel Patrice

Printed in China
First edition
1 3 5 6 4 2

CONTENTS

Barnyard Talk

Hens are clucking,
Roosters crowing,
Sheep are bleating,
Cattle lowing,

Pigs are oinking,
Horses neighing,
Geese are honking,
Donkeys braying,

Bulls are snorting,
Chicks are peeping,
Ducks are quacking . . .
I'm *not* sleeping!

STOMACH MATH

You and I have only one,
and one will surely do.
But cows need more, so they have four—
for them, one stomach's three too few.
Poor cow. When eating too much cake,
she has four times a bellyache.

8

WHEN PIGS COULD FLY

In a time when all piggies could fly,
They swooped and soared through the sky
Till below they saw MUD
And dropped with a **THUD**—
They have stayed ever since in a sty.

RECITE YOUR CHICKENS

Redcap, Rosecomb, Sultan, Dorking,
Frizzle, Plymouth Rock, Ancona,
Holland, Hamburg, Phoenix, Leghorn,
Cornish, Naked Neck, Lamona,

Chantecler and Delaware,
Jersey Giant, Buckeye, Brahma,
Orpington, Malay, and Campine,
Dominique and Yokohama,

Buttercup, Rhode Island Red—
That's enough! I'm going to bed!

FRISKY FILLY

Frisky filly in the field
kicking up her heels.
Old mare standing in the hay,
flicking summer flies away,
sighs, remembering the way
a frisky filly feels.

MAD MAGOG

To guard our hens
we need no dog—
we have a goose
called Mad Magog.

Birds stop singing,
bees stop humming
when they see
Magog is coming.

Magog is known
for chasing trucks,
scaring children,
biting ducks.

All the cows
takes off in fear—
RUN FOR YOUR LIFE!
Magog is here!

No fox in its
right mind would dare
come near our hens—
Magog is there!

THE ROOSTER CROWED AT MIDNIGHT

The Milky Way gave off such light,
the rooster crowed at twelve last night.

The moon looked so much like the sun,
he crowed again at half past one,

and then again at half past two
because right then the north wind blew.

A star shone high above a tree,
and so the rooster crowed at three.

He slept a bit, but then at four,
the rooster's crow rang out once more.

At five, he heard the cattle lowing,
and so, of course, he started crowing.

The farmer came at six o'clock
and put an end to that old cock.

HEADING HOME

Here come the cows all in a line
one
    by one
       by one
          by one
heading homeward, looking fine
in the glow of setting sun,
never varying their pace,
each one always in her place,
strolling home, her thoughts on hay,
day
    by day
       by day
         by day.

A Chicken Will Eat Most Anything

Eggshells, earwigs, spiders, slugs,
Salted peanuts, turnips, bugs,

Locusts, garbage, weeds, tomatoes,
Watermelon, sweet potatoes,

Crickets, sow bugs, centipedes,
Beetles, worms, all kinds of seeds,

Roaches, pizza, termites, lice—
A chicken thinks they're all quite nice.

No Rest

Their heads keep bobbing on their necks,
Every day a zillion pecks.
Scratching, scratching in the ground—
Each day a million bugs are found.
From dawn until the daylight ends,
There's never any rest for hens.

CHUCK'S DUCK

Chuck's in the muck.
"Where *is* that duck?"

Max hears a quack.
"She's under the shack—
go get the sack!"

Chuck sneaks to the shack,
opens the sack,
gets stuck in the muck,
but grabs the duck.

Duck thinks quick,
recalls a trick,
stretches her neck,
and takes a peck.
Chuck drops the duck
and yells, "Oh, heck!"

"Relax," says Max.
"I'll get my sax."

He blows some heat.
Those notes are sweet—
a

WHACK
THWACK
MANIAC
HACKENSACK
beat.

The awestruck duck
comes out—what luck!

LOVE

Our rooster has terrible luck.
He has fallen in love with a duck.
But the rooster can't swim,
And the chances are slim
That his sweetheart will ever speak **CLUCK**.

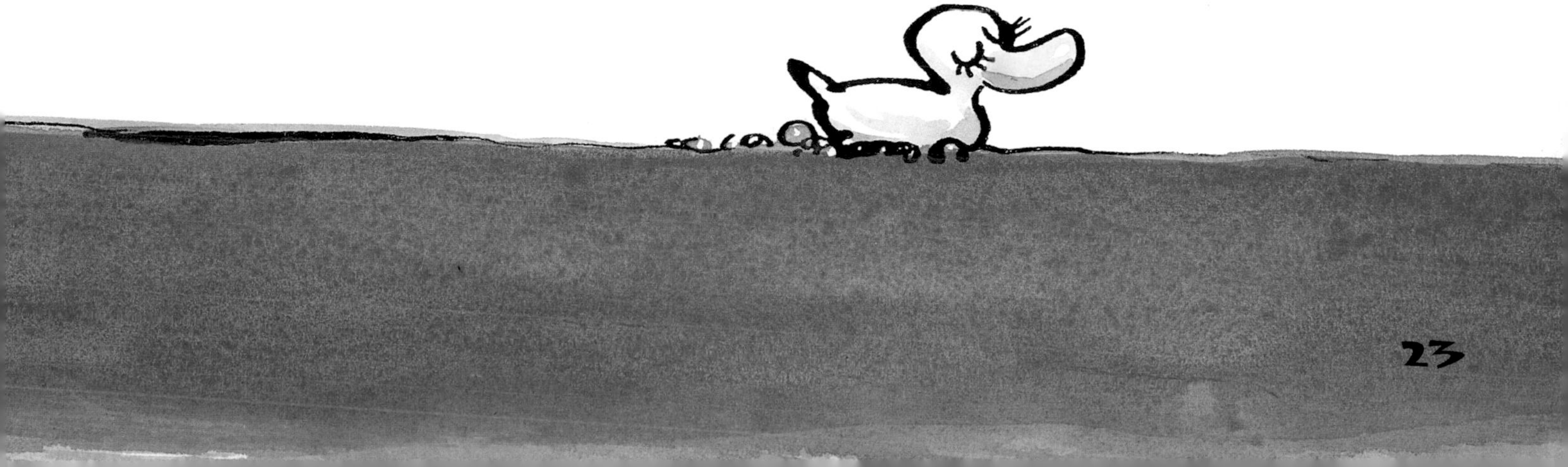

Jump Rope Rhyme

Call the doctor quick quick quick—
Our old pig is mighty sick.
If you can't get the doctor, call a nurse.
If you can't get a nurse, then call a hearse.
If our old piggy winds up dead,
We'll have some bacon with our bread.

COW DAZE

Spotted cows
mooing moos
minding their
p's and q's
chewing cud
swatting flies
watching bees
dropping pies.

GOATS ON THE ROOF

There are goats on the roof—
How'd they get way up there?
Did they swing through the trees?
Did they walk up a stair?
Did they drop from a plane?
Did they climb up the drain?
Did a hurricane blow them?
Did somebody throw them?
If ever you doubted
That goats are great jumpers,
Well, here is the proof:
There are goats on the roof!

My Dog

Hens give us eggs.
Pigs give us bacon.
Steer give us burgers,
if I'm not mistaken.

Sheep give us wool
to make sweaters and caps.
Geese give us down
to make pillows for naps.

Cows give us milk
for ice cream and cheese.
But my dog gives me kisses
and tail wags . . .

and fleas.

BARN CATS

Barn cats are howly.
They spit and they spat.
Barn cats are growly.
They rarely get fat—
They dine on the barn mice.
They're not very nice.

But barn-cat kittens are cuddly and soft.
They sleep in a jumble up in the loft,
Chase after dust motes, trip over their feet—
Barn-cat kittens are ever so sweet.

Winter Miracle

While looking at the sky last night
I saw a startling crowd:
A hundred sheep had taken flight.
It was a most amazing sight.

As they sailed from cloud to cloud
I heard a shepherd's horn
ring out in tones so true and proud,
the sheep stopped still, turned 'round, and bowed.

And then, as sure as I was born,
the shepherd's hand reached through
and sheared them all till they were shorn.
Their fleece fell down until the morn.

Today we woke to Earth made new,
all carpeted in white.
But I'm the only one who knew
last night a hundred white sheep flew.